Say What?

Margaret Peterson Haddix
Illustrated by James Bernardin

Aladdin Paperbacks
New York   London   Toronto   Sydney

ALADDIN PAPERBACKS
An imprint of Simon & Schuster Children's Publishing Division
1230 Avenue of the Americas, New York, NY 10020
Text copyright © 2004 by Margaret Peterson Haddix
Illustrations copyright © 2004 by James Bernardin
All rights reserved, including the right of reproduction
in whole or in part in any form.
ALADDIN PAPERBACKS and colophon are trademarks
of Simon & Schuster, Inc.
Also available in a Simon & Schuster Books for Young Readers
hardcover edition.
Designed by Mark Siegel
The text of this book was set in Utopia.
The illustrations were rendered in charcoal pencil on paper.
Manufactured in the United States of America
First Aladdin Paperbacks edition October 2005
8 10 9 7
The Library of Congress has cataloged the
hardcover edition as follows:
Haddix, Margaret Peterson.
Say what? / Margaret Peterson Haddix
p. cm.
Summary: When their parents begin saying the wrong thing
every time six-year-old Sukie and her older brothers misbehave,
the children discover that it is a plot and fight back with
their own wrong phrases.
ISBN-13: 978-0-689-86255-7 (hc.)
ISBN-10: 0-689-86255-5 (hc.)
[1. Behavior—Fiction. 2. Parenting—Fiction. 3. English language—
Terms and phrases—Fiction.] I. Title
PZ7.H1164 Say 2004
[Fic]—dc21   2002155512
ISBN-13: 978-0-689-86256-4 (Aladdin pbk.)
ISBN-10: 0-689-86256-3 (Aladdin pbk.)

For my own coconspirators, Bob, John, and Janet;
and my parents, who put up with us;
but most of all, for Meredith and Connor

With thanks to Janis Shannon and Barbara Munn
for their expert advice

CHAPTER 1

Sukie Rose Robinson was running through the living room with a big plastic tub of glitter in each hand.

All right, Sukie *knew* she was doing something wrong. She was only six years old, but Mom and Dad had already told her at least ten billion times, "No running in the house. This isn't a playground." And they'd told her at least five billion times, "You have to ask before you use glitter. And *only* at the kitchen table."

But Sukie wasn't trying to be bad. She was just in a hurry. She'd been making tissue-paper flowers in her room, and she'd thought of a cool way to put glitter on all the petals. She didn't have time to hunt up Mom or Dad and ask permission, or to move all her flowers to the kitchen. She had to get the glitter before she forgot her great idea—

Oh, no! Dad saw her!

Busted!

Dad was walking from the kitchen to the family room, a coffee cup in his hand. His eyebrows went up when his eyes met Sukie's. Sukie *tried* to slow down, to make it look like she'd just been strolling along, no faster than a snail. She tried to hide the tubs of glitter behind her back, real fast. But her shoulders were bent forward, her legs were kicked straight out. It wasn't like she could just stop. She braced herself for the usual, "Sukie! How many times have we told you not to run in the house? And what's that in your hands?"

But instead, Dad frowned at her and said, "If all your friends jumped off a bridge, would you jump off a bridge too?"

Huh?

Confused, Sukie skidded to a halt. The two tubs of glitter crashed into each other behind her back. Sukie tried to hold her hands steady, but the tubs tilted and the lids slipped off. The tops on the individual shakers of glitter inside the tubs must have been loose. Sukie looked over her shoulder and saw a whole waterfall of green and gold and red and purple and orange glitter streaming down to the carpet.

Sukie hunched over. Now Dad was really going to yell. "What do you think you're doing, young lady?" he was going to say. "Why do you have glitter in the living room? Do you know how long it's going to take *you* to clean that up?"

But Dad didn't yell. Not right away.

Sukie looked up at him, waiting.

Dad was taking a deep breath. Then he looked her straight in the eye and said, "Don't pick your nose. That's a gross habit."

And then he walked on, into the family room, sipping his coffee.

Sukie hadn't been picking her nose. Who would pick their nose with their hands full of glitter?

Sukie stared after Dad. She dropped the tubs of glitter, and even more spilled out on the carpet. Sukie stepped over it and peeked in at Dad in the family room. He was reading the newspaper and drinking his coffee, just like nothing had happened.

Sukie tiptoed back to the living room. She tugged and pulled and shoved the rocking chair over the pile of glitter on the carpet. Then she hid the glitter tubs under the couch. She didn't feel like making glitter-flowers anymore.

This was too weird. What was wrong with Dad?

CHAPTER 2

NOBODY SAID ANYTHING about glitter at dinner. But something else strange happened.

They were having meat loaf and peas. Sukie hated peas. Really, peas didn't taste any worse than any other vegetable. But they were too hard to eat.

Her oldest brother, Brian, who was nine, had told her, "Just use your spoon like a shovel. Scoop them up." But if Sukie did that, one or two of the peas always escaped and rolled off her plate, and then Mom or Dad yelled at her. One time when they'd had company, Sukie had even shot a pea into Mr. Harbinger's lap. Then when Sukie started laughing, peas she hadn't swallowed yet had dropped out of her mouth and—

Well, she'd gotten into a lot of trouble for that one.

Sukie's other brother, Reed, who was seven, had given her different advice for eating peas.

"Just stab them right in the eye," he'd said. "Pretend your fork's a sword, see, and the peas are dragons you've got to kill, and you're a famous knight, and the peas kind of squeal a little when they die. . . ."

Sukie didn't mind playing with her food. But she just couldn't see spending her whole life stabbing one pea at a time, whether they squealed or not.

Really, if Sukie were in charge of the whole wide world, she'd pass a law that said peas were finger food, like potato chips or carrots, and people had to eat them with their hands. If anyone even picked up a fork or a spoon around a pea—

boom!—Sukie would have them thrown in jail.

But Sukie would never be in charge of the whole wide world. Not with Brian and Reed and Mom and Dad telling her what to do.

Tonight she bent down really low beside her plate and cupped her left hand so she could hide her right hand grabbing up the peas and sticking them in her mouth.

But Mom saw. Of course Mom saw.

"Sukie!"

Sukie thought, *It's not my fault my left hand's not big enough to hide what my right hand's doing.*

But Mom didn't yell, "Don't eat with your fingers!" Instead, she scolded, "You'll put an eye out with that thing!"

"Huh?" Sukie said.

And this time she really wanted Mom to

give her the whole lecture, about how table manners were important, and how they showed respect for the other people eating with her, and how could Mom and Dad let Sukie grow up eating like she lived in a barn? It would almost make Sukie feel good to be yelled at like that.

But Mom just frowned at her the same way Dad had, and said, "Lying is not acceptable in this household, young lady."

Sukie dropped her peas and scrunched down on her seat. This wasn't just weird. This was scary. This was too scary for a six-year-old to handle all by herself. She kicked Brian under the table. She needed his help.

Quit that!" Brian snarled. "Mo-om! Sukie's kicking me!"

All right, Sukie thought. *Now.* Now Mom would say, "Sukie, quit kicking Brian.

Brian, don't tattle on your sister." And if she didn't, Brian would notice, and he would say, "Whoa, Mom. What's wrong with you?"

"Waste not, want not," Mom said, and took a bite of meat loaf.

Brian didn't even seem to hear Mom. He just went right back to talking to Reed about how PlayStations were better than Nintendos.

"Um, Mom," Sukie said, "do you feel okay?"

"Sure," Mom said. "Would you pass the peas, please?"

Well, that proved that Mom still knew how to say *something* that made sense. Or maybe not. Who in their right mind would *ask* for peas?

CHAPTER 3

BRIAN DIDN'T SEE ANY REASON why he had to have a younger sister. So when Sukie knocked on his door after dinner and yelled, "Brian, let me in! I've got to talk to you!" he said what he always said: "Go away!"

Every time he said that, Sukie would get her feelings all hurt, and then she'd go crying to Mom or Dad, and then Mom or Dad would come and give him some big lecture about how Sukie was the only sister he had, and she looked up to him, and someday when he was a grown-up, he'd appreciate her. . . .

Blah, blah, blah, blah, blah. It went on forever.

But it was still worth getting that lecture if it meant he could have five more minutes without Sukie bugging him. Five minutes was how long it usually took her to go tattle to Mom and Dad. He knew. He'd timed it.

"Go away!" he yelled again, just in case Sukie hadn't heard him. He sat down on his bed and tossed a miniature basketball at the plastic hoop he'd rigged up over his door. This was a good way to work on his close-angle shots since his bed was right beside the door.

"No, listen. I've got to tell you something. It's important," Sukie said.

Important to Sukie was something like, "Look, I braided this Barbie's hair, and this other Barbie's hair is still straight down. Don't you think the braided one looks better?" Brian leaned back on his bed to catch his basketball. It bounced perfectly into his hands. He threw it again.

"I don't care!" he yelled back to Sukie. "I said, 'Go away.'"

"No!" Sukie said. "You have to listen to me!"

Brian caught his basketball and threw it again. He couldn't hear Sukie's footsteps retreating from his door yet.

He rolled forward on the bed, unlocked the door and poked his face out to glare at Sukie. That *always* worked.

The basketball hit him smack on the back of his head. Sukie giggled. Brian glared harder, but she still didn't budge.

Brian relaxed his glaring muscles.

"Isn't it time for you to run off and go

tattle to Mom and Dad?" he asked. "What's wrong with you?"

"Nothing's wrong with me," Sukie said. "Something's wrong with them. Mom and Dad. They're not acting normal."

"Well, sure. They're grown-ups. You can't expect grown-ups to act normal."

"But they're acting really, really weird. Haven't you noticed?" Sukie asked. She sounded scared.

Brian thought for a minute. He'd seen Dad outside mowing the yard that morning, wearing orange-and-brown plaid shorts. He'd heard Mom talking back to some chef on TV—"No, wait, how much tarragon did you use?"—like she really thought the chef could hear her.

"No weirder than usual," Brian said, shrugging. It took a lot of talent to shrug while lying on a bed and leaning your head halfway out the door. It took even more talent to look dignified while shrugging and lying down and leaning out a door. Brian decided he'd better quit while he was ahead. He scrambled off his bed and stood up. He grabbed the doorknob.

"So now you've talked to me," he told Sukie. "Now scram."

He started to shut the door, but Sukie was really quick and stuck her foot between the door and the doorframe. Brian would never have told her, but he was kind of impressed. He'd never seen anybody do that before except on TV detective shows.

"We've got to have an all-kid meeting," Sukie said.

Whoa. This was serious. The last time they'd had an all-kid meeting was when their dog died. Brian narrowed his eyes.

"I'm the only one who can call an all-kid meeting," he said, just in case Sukie was getting any big ideas.

"I know," Sukie said. "That's why I'm asking you to call one."

She smiled up at him sweetly, just like she smiled at Mom and Dad when she wanted ice cream or candy or the first choice of what ride to go on when they went to an amusement park. Mom and Dad always fell for it, but *he* wasn't going to. At least, not without making her suffer first.

"What'll you give me?" he asked.

"My allowance for the next two weeks," Sukie said. "And I'll make your bed for you every day this month."

Okay, she was serious. She was even scaring Brian a little bit.

"All right," Brian said. "Fine. Go tell

Reed I said for him to come in here now."

She whirled around and left so quickly he thought he'd messed up. The way she was acting, she probably would have given him her whole year's worth of allowance.

CHAPTER 4

REED WAS GETTING READY for the Greatest Battle in the Universe on his bedroom floor. Batman, Superman, Spider-Man and all his McDonald's Happy Meal knights were on one side. Cubeman, his old Fisher-Price dragon, and every action figure he'd ever gotten from Burger King or Wendy's were on the other side. He was trying to figure out if some of the Burger King guys might switch sides, when suddenly Sukie was there shouting right in his ear, "BRIAN SAYS WE HAVE TO HAVE A KID MEETING IN HIS ROOM! RIGHT NOW!"

Reed blinked at his little sister.

"You don't have to yell," he said.

"Yes, I do," Sukie said. "You didn't hear me the first six times."

Reed shrugged. Now she sounded like Mom and Dad. They yelled at him all the time, "Reed, pay attention!" "Reed, stop daydreaming!" "Reed, weren't you listening?"

Reed figured, if real life was ever interesting enough, he'd be glad to pay attention. Until then—well, what if the Wendy's action figures were the traitors, instead of the Burger King ones? He started to move one gruesome-faced plastic figure to the other side of the room.

"REED!" Sukie yelled.

"Okay!" Reed said, reluctantly getting up. He glared sternly at Cubeman. "Now don't start fighting until I get back, you hear?"

He followed Sukie down the hall.

CHAPTER 5

BRIAN SAT ON HIS BED cross-legged, keeping his back ramrod straight, like a king. He made Reed and Sukie sit on the floor in front of him. They were lucky he was even letting them in his room.

"This had better be good," Reed said. "And quick. Or else the Greatest Battle in the Universe isn't going to start on time."

Brian ignored him.

"The all-kid meeting will now come to order," he said. "You there. Did you have something to report?"

Sukie stood up.

"You know my name," she complained. "Why don't you use it instead of calling me 'you there'?"

Brian ignored that comment too.

"State your business," Brian said, just like he'd seen a king do one time on TV. Really, all he needed was a crown.

Sukie rolled her eyes.

"It's like I told you. Mom and Dad are acting weird. They keep saying the wrong things. Dad saw me running in the house and he said, 'If all your friends jumped off a bridge, would you jump off a bridge?' and then I spilled a little glitter—well, a lot of glitter—and he said, 'Don't pick your nose,' and I wasn't. My hands weren't even anywhere close to my nose. They were practically in another room from my nose."

Her voice was getting higher and higher, like she was panicking.

"And then at dinner," Sukie continued, "I was eating my peas with my fingers—"

"After picking your nose?" Brian couldn't help interrupting.

"I told you, I didn't pick my nose!"

"Never? Never ever in your entire life?" Brian challenged, forgetting he was trying to act haughty and regal, like a king. "Cross your heart and hope to die, stick a needle in your eye?"

"Well, not today, I mean. Not before dinner." Sukie looked down guiltily. "Anyway, that's not what I wanted to talk about. It's Mom and Dad. I was eating my peas with my fingers and Mom didn't yell at me the right way. She said, 'You could put an eye out with that thing,' and that's just wrong, that's the wrong thing to say, peas aren't pointy at all—"

"Maybe she meant you could've poked your eye out when you were picking your nose," Reed said. "You could, I bet. If you missed your nose and you poked your finger in your eye, and it was going really fast, and your fingernail was really long, like that guy in the *Guinness Book of World Records,* or maybe not quite that long, because his fingernails curl around. You'd need your fingernails to be really, really sharp and pointy—"

"I WASN'T PICKING MY NOSE! I WAS EATING PEAS!" Sukie yelled.

Brian looked at Reed and Reed looked at Brian. Brian knew that his brother was thinking the exact same thing he was: In a minute, Sukie was going to start crying. And then Mom and Dad would be in here yelling at him and Reed, and it just wouldn't be fair.

"Okay, okay," Brian said quickly. "Let the record show that no nose picking took place at dinner." He liked "Let the record show" even though no one was taking notes. He'd heard a judge say that on TV once. Maybe it'd be better to be a judge instead of a king. Kings had to wear girly-looking robes. And those crowns might be painful. Brian sat up even straighter and tried to look serious and somber, like a TV judge. "The witness may sit down," he said sternly to Sukie.

Sukie didn't move. She seemed frozen, midyell, right on the edge of a tantrum.

"That's you, Sukie," Brian said. "You can sit down. You're the witness. That's better than 'you there,' isn't it?"

Sukie took a deep gulp of air and said in a small voice, "So what are you going to do about Mom and Dad? How are you going to fix them?"

Brian hadn't thought about that at all. The way Sukie was looking at him, with her eyes all big and trusting—well, it was almost like she did believe he was as powerful as a king, as wise as a judge. It wouldn't be so bad having a little sister if she'd always look at him that way.

Except he didn't know what to do about Mom and Dad. He was almost twice as old as Sukie, and he didn't know any better than she did why they might be acting weird.

"Hmm," he said. "I believe we need more evidence. You there. Have you noticed Mom and Dad saying the wrong things?"

He was talking to Reed, but Reed just kept staring off into space. Sukie poked him in the side.

"REED! BRIAN ASKED YOU A QUESTION! HAVE MOM AND DAD SAID ANYTHING WEIRD TO YOU?" she yelled.

Reed blinked at her, like he'd just arrived from Pluto and hadn't quite adjusted to Earth.

"Um, I don't know," he said. "I don't usually listen to them." He looked up at Brian. "Have they said anything weird to you?"

Brian frowned and admitted, "I don't pay much attention either. It's always the same thing. 'Clean your room.' 'Be nice to your sister.' 'Do your homework.' Every word that comes out of their mouths I've already heard a billion times. But Sukie, she's little. She's dumb enough to think they might actually say something new."

"I am not!" Sukie said.

"Are too!" Brian said.

"Am n— Wait a minute. I was right this time. They are saying different stuff. So there." She stuck her tongue out at Brian.

"Okay, okay," Brian said quickly. He was

sure that real kings and judges didn't have to put up with people sticking out their tongues at them. "Here's what we've got to do. We've got to gather evidence."

"Huh?" Sukie said.

"We've got to be bad. On purpose."

Chapter 6

REED SPENCER ROBINSON, the world famous spy, had his back pressed tightly against a wall. Or—wait a minute—how could a spy be world famous? If everybody knew who he was, he wouldn't be a very good spy, would he? Maybe his name was famous, but nobody had ever seen his face. Maybe he was a master of disguise. Yeah, that was it.

"Hey, Reed. Whatcha doing?" It was Dad.

Oh, no. Caught already. Reed Spencer Robinson, world-renowned master of disguise, jumped away from the wall. Then he smiled a crafty smile. Reed Spencer Robinson, famous spy, knew how to turn around any situation. He, Brian, and Sukie had agreed that they would try to get Mom and Dad to yell at them, and see what they said. This was a perfect opportunity.

"I'm putting handprints on the wall," Reed said. "As many as possible."

Handprints were a big no-no in the Robinson household. The way Mom and Dad acted, you'd think a single smudge on the wall was the crime of the century.

"Handprints?" Dad's eyes seemed to bug out a little.

"Yeah," Reed said. "And then I'm going to go smear my fingers on every window in the house."

That should do it. Dad's eyes just had to bug out a little bit more, and then he'd be yelling about how much work it took to keep a house clean, and how everyone in the house needed to help out and that meant . . . Well, Reed wasn't sure what the rest of the lecture was, because he'd never

paid attention before. But he was ready to pay attention now.

Dad seemed to gulp, and then he said, "Eat your vegetables." And walked away.

Reed whipped out the little notebook he'd tucked in his back pocket and wrote down, "Handprince—eat vejibuls." He wasn't sure he'd spelled all the words right, but, hey, even a world-famous spy couldn't be good at everything.

CHAPTER 7

I

T WAS EVEN WORSE than Brian had thought.

He, Reed, and Sukie were having their second kid meeting in two days. They'd spent the past twenty-four hours doing everything they could to get Mom and Dad to yell at them the right way. Brian had spilled orange juice all over the kitchen floor, but instead of saying, "Clean it up," Mom had said, "Shut the door. You think we can afford to air-condition the whole outdoors?"

Sukie had coughed right in Dad's face without covering her mouth, a dozen times, and all Dad said was, "Money doesn't grow on trees, you know."

Reed had worn his muddy shoes into

the living room, with its stupid cream-colored carpet that Mom was always so worried about, and all Mom had said was, "I don't care who started it. I'm stopping it."

Brian sorted through the notes littering his bed, most of them in Reed's bad handwriting.

"Look here," Brian said. "Dad even said, 'Use your words,' when I was bouncing the basketball in the family room."

"What's 'Use your words' mean?" Sukie asked.

"Don't you remember?" Brian said. "Mom and Dad used to say that all the time when you were really little and you'd get mad and start hitting Reed or me. You used to bite Reed too. It never made sense to me. When you started saying, 'I hate you! You're mean!' instead of hitting or biting, they'd give you a time-out for that, too."

"Oh," Sukie said. "I didn't remember that."

Brian kind of expected her to say, "You're making it up, right? I'm sure I never bit anyone. Not me." Because that's how girls were. Prissy. But she didn't say it. She just sat there looking white faced and worried.

Strange how that bothered Brian. It was bad when even Sukie wasn't acting normal anymore.

Reed reached up for the stack of notes Brian had taken.

"I bet I know why Mom and Dad are acting weird," he said, looking at the notes.

"Why?" Sukie asked eagerly.

"They're really robots," Reed said. "Maybe they've always been robots, but we never noticed before. But now their voice boxes got scrambled, so they're saying all the wrong things. We just need to have them taken back to the robot shop and get their voice boxes fixed. Or maybe—I just thought of this—maybe our real mom and dad have been kidnapped by aliens, and the aliens replaced them with fakes that look just like our real mom and dad, except the aliens messed up on the voice command, and—"

"I DON'T WANT ROBOTS! I DON'T WANT ALIENS! I WANT MY REAL MOMMY AND DADDY!" Sukie yelled.

Brian dived off the bed and clapped his hand over Sukie's mouth. At the same time, Reed reached over to shut her up too. So they ended up, all three of them, in a giant pile on the floor. Brian had both hands over Sukie's mouth and so did Reed.

"Stop it! You're scaring her!" Brian said.

"It's not my fault our parents have

turned into robots or aliens," Reed argued. He had that look in his eye that meant he was going to keep talking, and probably say something even scarier.

Brian took one hand off Sukie's mouth and clamped it over Reed's.

"Listen," Brian said. "I'm the oldest kid. What I say goes. In a crisis like this, it doesn't do any good to panic. We have to be calm. You have to do what I say."

"Unt oo uu unt uh oo oo?" Sukie grunted. But she grunted calmly, so Brian removed his hand. Reed did too.

"What do you want us to do?" Sukie repeated quietly.

Oops. Brian hadn't thought of that.

Then he heard Mom yell from out in the living room, "Kids! Bedtime!"

Brian felt the relief wash over him. It was kind of nice to hear Mom say something that made sense, even if she was telling them to go to bed. And this saved him from having to come up with some brilliant plan right away.

"That's it," Brian said. "I don't have time to give you your orders tonight. *Think* when you go to bed. We'll rendezvous again in the morning."

He could tell from their blank expressions that Sukie and Reed had no idea what "rendezvous" meant. He wasn't so sure himself, but he'd heard a general say that once in a war movie.

A general. Hmm. Maybe that was the right role for Brian. . . .

CHAPTER 8

REED SPENCER ROBINSON, the famous spy, was out of bed. He tiptoed down the hall, keeping an eagle eye out for the telltale red lines of the laser security system.

Okay. Really, he just had to make sure that he didn't step on any of the toys he, Brian, and Sukie had left littering the hall.

Reed was feeling bad that he'd scared Sukie. He thought it'd be fun if Mom and Dad were really robots or aliens. Think how jealous all the other kids at school would be!

But if it frightened Sukie so much— well, then, it was up to Reed to find out the truth.

Reed reached the end of the hall and

silently slipped down onto his hands and knees. He inched forward, quiet as a cat. It was hard to say what Reed Spencer Robinson was most famous for: his disguises or his ability to slip in and out of dangerous places unseen. Maybe he was known as the "Invisible Spy." Yeah, that was it.

"Think the hooligans are asleep yet?" Dad was saying to Mom in the family room.

"I'll go check," Mom said.

Oh, no! Alert! Alert! Mom was coming this way!

With lightning speed, Reed rolled around and dove under the kitchen table. He bonked his head on one of the table legs but Reed Spencer Robinson, the Invisible Spy, knew better than to cry out in pain. Even torture couldn't make him talk. What was a little bump on the head compared with torture?

Mom walked right by without even looking down. Reed lay absolutely still, barely even breathing. A moment later she walked past again and reported to Dad, "Yep. They're all out like logs."

Reed grinned silently, delighted that he'd thought to leave a body-sized lump of pillows under the covers in his bed.

"They should be sleeping," Dad said bitterly, "after all the ways they misbehaved today. I swear, Sandy, this plan of yours is backfiring. The kids are breaking more rules than ever."

Plan? Plan?

Reed felt like his ears were snapping to attention, like antennae shooting up. For maybe the first time in his life, he had no desire whatsoever to start daydreaming. He listened intently.

"We just need to be patient," Mom said.

Reed raised his head ever so slightly. Through a maze of chair and table legs, he could see Mom picking up a magazine from the coffee table.

"See, it says in the article: 'Some parents may experience a brief spell of increased rebellion or disobedience from their offspring, as children are puzzled by the unusual commands. But within days, children will be begging you, "No, no, tell me to pick up my clothes off the floor. Look, I'm doing what I'm supposed to." Children secretly crave rules and order.'" She lowered the magazine. "I really do think they're paying attention now. They're listening every time we say the wrong thing. Even Reed, and when was the last time he listened to anything?"

Reed felt a little insulted by that. He did listen to what other people said *sometimes*.

Just not when it was boring.

Dad groaned.

"I guess you're right," he said. "But I keep feeling like I'm going to crack before they do. I just can't think of enough wrong things to say. I caught Reed making hand-prints on the wall, and it was all I could do to come up with 'Eat your vegetables.'"

"That's a good one," Mom said comfortingly. "I actually told Sukie 'Waste not, want not,' last night at dinner. I don't think my grandmother even said that. Here. Let's look at the list in the magazine again together. Let's see, there's the 'would you jump off a bridge?' one—"

"Used it already," Dad muttered.

"Um, 'Money doesn't grow on trees.' 'If I've told you once, I've told you a thousand times . . .' Oh, here's one we haven't said lately. 'If you're bored, I can think of plenty of chores for you to do.' That's a good one, don't you think?"

"Yeah, I guess," Dad said. "But I'm too tired to think about this right now. Why don't we just watch TV?"

He flipped on the set, and a toothpaste commercial sprang onto the screen. Mom put the magazine back on the coffee table. It slipped over to the edge—the edge farthest from Mom and Dad.

Reed Spencer Robinson, the Invisible Spy and Master of Disguises, had a mission. He was going after that magazine. It would take every ounce of skill he had—but, hey, wasn't he the most skillful spy on the planet?

Slowly, under the cover of the TV noise, he scooted one of the chairs out of his way. Then he crept forward on his elbows and belly, keeping down as low as possible. In seconds he was at the edge of the family room carpet. He circled around behind the couch his parents were on. So far, so good.

Reed waited, gathering nerve for his next move, the most dangerous of all. Slowly he reached around from behind the couch. Closer, closer—his fingers were only inches away from the magazine. Then his fingertips brushed the edge of the magazine pages. He just had to pull it away quietly—

Blomp!

The magazine slipped out of his grasp and down to the floor. The noise seemed to drown out the TV. Reed jerked his hand back immediately. If he'd had a walkie-talkie like a real spy, he'd be screaming into it, "Mayday! Mayday! Abort mission! Switch to rescuing spy from enemy territory!" He waited for Mom or Dad to

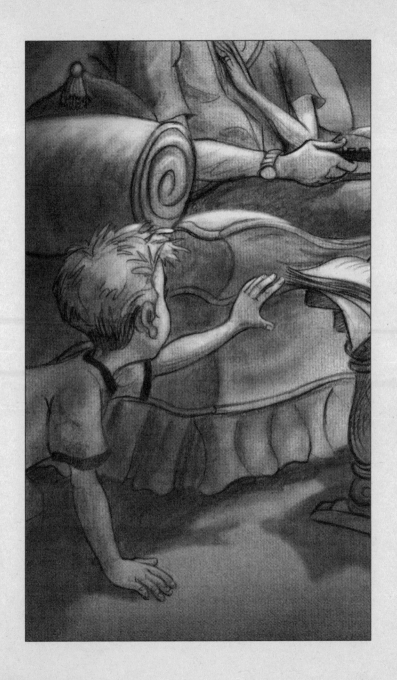

pick up the magazine, to look behind the couch and scream out, "Young man, what are you doing out of bed?"

Nothing happened.

Nothing happened for a very long time.

Reed waited through a soup commercial and a very dull song on VH1. Then he cautiously raised his head and peeked over the top of the couch.

Mom and Dad were cuddled together, sound asleep.

Sometimes a world-famous spy needs skill. And sometimes he just gets lucky.

Reed stood all the way up, walked around the couch, and picked up the magazine. He thought about whistling as he walked away, but decided against it. No need to push his luck.

CHAPTER 9

SUKIE WAS JUST SETTLING into a very pleasant dream where mommies and daddies acted like they were supposed to, and the sun shone every day, and flowers bloomed everywhere. Oh, and little girls all had as many Barbie dolls as they wanted . . .

Then someone was shaking her and whispering, "Wake up! You've got to wake up!"

"Why?" Sukie murmured.

"Read this!" Reed shoved something at her face and turned on the light.

Sukie had barely started kindergarten. So far all she could read was her name and a few words that had just two or three letters, like "get" and "out." She didn't see any of those words in the magazine Reed was thrusting at her, but she said them anyway. "Get out of my room, Reed. I'm sleeping!"

"Not now, you aren't," Reed said. "Don't you see? I've solved the puzzle! I know the real reason that Mom and Dad are acting weird!"

"It's not worse than aliens or robots, is it?" Sukie asked, scrunching down in her pillow.

"No, no, they're just doing some stupid experiment from a magazine. Come on— we've got to go tell Brian."

Secretly Sukie was pleased that Reed had told her before Brian. Though she did kind of miss seeing what was going to happen in her dream with all those flowers and Barbie dolls. She followed Reed out of her room and into Brian's.

Brian was very hard to wake up. He kept

rolling around in his covers and crying out, "Advance! Advance! We've got to be braver than the enemy!" Finally Sukie had to poke him in the side and warn him, "Brian! You're going to get Mom and Dad in here yelling at us, and how can we hold a kid meeting then?"

Brian sat up, blinking.

"I call all the kid meetings," he said.

"So call one, already," Sukie said.

Brian blinked again, and said, "This meeting will now come to order. Does anyone have any—"

Reed didn't wait for Brian to finish his question. "I solved the mystery! I solved the mystery! See, it's all in this magazine—"

Brian tore the magazine out of Reed's hands.

"*New Ways of Parenting*," he read from the cover. "What kind of a stupid magazine is this?"

"Look, it's this article," Reed said, shoving pages between Brian's fingers.

Sukie let the boys yank the magazine back and forth, and waited for them to read it. She'd already decided the magazine had ugly pictures, so *she* didn't need to see it.

Somehow the two boys found the right article and were poring over it together.

"'Children secretly crave rules and order'?" Brian read aloud, like he couldn't believe what he was seeing.

"What's 'crave' mean?" Sukie asked.

"That you want something really, really bad," Brian said.

"Rules and order?" Sukie said. "Bleck. Are you sure they don't mean 'hate'?"

But Brian was shaking his head. He and Reed kept reading. Every once in a while, one of them would yell out, "Oh, no, this is crazy!" or, "That's not true!"

Sukie threaded her fingers together and played a little game twirling one thumb around the other. Finally she was sure she'd waited long enough.

"Aren't you going to tell me anything?" she begged.

Brian looked up. His hair was sticking up all over the place because he kept tearing his hands through it every time he cried out, "Oh, man, that's so wrong!"

"It's all a plot, see. They're trying to turn us into perfectly behaved children," he said. "It's just—well, here's how the article starts out."

And then he ripped the magazine from Reed's grasp and read straight from the article, in his most mocking voice:

"'Do you have to remind your children six or seven times to pick up their toys—

and they still don't do it? Do you have to scold them again and again and again for the same misbehavior—and you still don't feel like they've heard you? Many modern parents complain of these problems. But only *New Ways* offers a scientifically proven solution . . .'"

Brian's eyes skimmed down the rest of the article.

"Then there's a bunch of blah, blah, blahing about what a genius the guy who developed this plan was," Brian said.

"What *is* the plan?" Sukie asked.

"It's just what Mom and Dad have been doing to us," Brian said. "You know. Saying the wrong things at the wrong times. They've even got this whole chart of what they call 'Parentspeak Phrases'—'No dessert until you eat your vegetables' . . . yep, they say that . . . 'No running with scissors' . . . yep, they say that . . ."

Sukie didn't want to listen to Brian saying all the things her parents already said all the time.

"But why?" Sukie said. "Why would they say the wrong things at the wrong time? Why say, 'No dessert until you eat your vegetables' if no one's eating? What if the real problem is that one of us is about to poke an eye out with a stick? If they're not saying the right thing, we might go ahead and poke the stick in our eye!"

"It's just temporary," Brian said. "To surprise us, because they don't think we've been listening. To catch us off guard. To turn us around so we're good all the time. Look, it says right here, 'Within days your little monsters will be magically transformed into little angels, eager to please, and delighted to have you scold them in your old, familiar manner.'"

Sukie thought about that. It would kind of be nice now to have Mom or Dad say the right things at the right times again. In fact, that's what she'd gone to bed longing for. But that was because she was afraid they'd been turned into aliens or robots. Now that she knew they were just trying to trick her and Brian and Reed, it made her mad. She narrowed her eyes and clenched her jaw and burst out, "That's not fair! They're being mean!"

"Yeah!" Brian agreed. "You said it, Sukie. This is—this is cruel and unusual punishment!"

"But what can we do about it?" Reed said.

Sukie looked up at both of her brothers. She couldn't believe their faces were blank, like they didn't have any ideas at all inside those seven- and nine-year-old brains of theirs.

"Well, duh," Sukie said. "We're going to do the same thing back to them."

CHAPTER 10

BRIAN STARED at his little sister. What made her think Reed and Brian would do something she suggested?

Still, it wasn't a bad idea. . . .

"But we're not like grown-ups," Reed was arguing. "We don't go around saying the same boring things all the time. *I* don't."

"You do so," Sukie said.

"Do not!"

"Do too!"

"Do—"

"There!" Brian said, grabbing a piece of paper and scribbling down four words. "That's a good one."

"Huh?" Reed said.

"That 'do too, do not' stuff. It drives

grown-ups crazy. That can be one of the things we say at the wrong time, when Mom and Dad say the wrong things to us."

"Oh," Reed said. He frowned. "Okay, maybe that one'll work. But that's the only thing we say all the time. Everything else we say is . . . original. Full of imagination."

Brian knew that was what Reed's teachers always said about him. Those words—"original . . . full of imagination"— came home on every single one of Reed's report cards.

"No, it isn't," Sukie said. "You say the same things over and over again all the time. Like if you tell me to do something, and I say, 'Make me,' you say, 'I don't have the recipe.' Always. Every single time."

"Then there's that stupid 'spell it' trick," Brian said. "Remember? You say, 'What's your name? Spell it.'"

Sukie nodded.

"And if I say, 'S-U-K-I-E,' you say, 'No, stupid, "it" is I-T.' But if I say, 'I-T,' you say, 'Your name's "it"? That's a funny name!'" Sukie made a face at Reed.

"That game is so second grade," Brian said scornfully.

"I am in second grade," Reed said in a small voice. He pushed his bottom lip out glumly. The way he looked, if he'd been Sukie's age, he would have been crying by now.

"Hey, it's all right," Brian said quickly. "We're just collecting a list of things we can say to drive Mom and Dad as crazy as they're driving us. That's a good one. Can you guys think of any others?"

"How about, 'But Connor's parents let him'?" Reed said slowly.

"Great!" Brian said.

"'I didn't mean to,'" Sukie said.

"Huh?" Brian said.

"For the *list*," Sukie said.

"Oh," Brian said. He wrote it down. And then Reed had a good idea, and Sukie had another one, and Brian had one himself. . . . In a matter of minutes the page was covered, and he was grabbing for more paper. They had all sorts of ammunition to hurl back at Mom and Dad.

Brian remembered imagining himself as a general. It was like he had suddenly, magically, become one.

This was war.

CHAPTER 11

THE WAR started slowly. The next day was Monday, and they had school. But everyone overslept. As Brian and Reed and Sukie scrambled into their clothes and gobbled down their breakfast and ran for the school bus, Mom and Dad didn't have time to say anything at all to them except, "Hurry up!"

What if the experiment was over?

Brian actually felt disappointed at that thought. It was like spending hours making a huge snow fort and dozens of snowballs for a snowball fight you were sure you were going to win, and then having the kids on the other side say, "You know what? We don't want to play after all. We're just going to go inside and watch TV."

But then after school, after both Mom and Dad were home from work, Brian was lying on his stomach on the couch doing his math homework. Mom walked by and glanced at him, and Brian suddenly remembered that he still had his shoes on.

What's more, he had his feet resting on the couch pillow that Mom always liked to lean against when she was watching TV.

And maybe his shoes were just the littlest bit muddy from recess.

Okay, they were caked with huge clumps of mud, because he'd been playing football at recess, and he'd scored a touchdown, and how was he to know there was a huge puddle in the end zone? He'd been running too fast to see it.

When Mom saw Brian with his muddy shoes on her favorite pillow, Brian could tell she was about to scream, "Brian! Get your shoes off the couch this instant! How many times do I have to tell you that? You clean that up right now! You're grounded, buddy!" Brian could see by her face that she was struggling to bite back those words. Instead she said, almost mildly, "Don't talk with your mouth full."

Brian gulped. This was it. His first chance. He narrowed his eyes and pictured the long, long list he and Reed and Sukie had made the night before. And then he shot back, "Sukie started it!"

Mom stared at him.

Brian saw the confusion in her eyes. He forced himself to stare straight back at her. He kept his expression as innocent as possible.

And then Mom whirled on her heels and walked away.

Yes! Brian had won the first battle. Brian

was so excited, he took his feet off the couch. He jumped up and did the same kind of touchdown dance he'd seen NFL players do on TV.

Oops. That left piles of dried mud everywhere.

But he was the victor, so he could afford to be a little generous. He got out the Dustbuster and vacuumed up the dried mud—even from the couch. And he took his shoes off before he ran to tell Reed and Sukie the good news.

CHAPTER 12

BY DINNERTIME anyone watching the Robinson family from outside would have thought that every single one of them had been replaced by robots with scrambled voice circuits.

Reed forgot to put the silverware on when he was setting the table, and instead of simply reminding him, Dad said, "Have you brushed your teeth?"

Reed replied, "Sukie's bugging me," though Sukie wasn't even in the kitchen. Sukie was in the family room telling Mom, "Nobody told me!" when Mom said, "Act your age!"

And all Sukie had done was trip and fall when she was running around the room. If you asked Reed, she was acting her age.

Brian kicked his soccer ball in the living room, and Dad told him, "This isn't a restaurant. Get it yourself."

And Brian answered, "I'm bored! There's nothing to do!"

Reed left his action figures spread across the kitchen floor, but instead of telling him to pick them up, Mom said, "How would you feel if someone called you 'stupid'?"

Reed replied, "Can I have dessert now?"

Reed loved it. Nobody made any sense at all.

This was better than pretending to be a spy. This was better than staging the Greatest Battle in the Universe between Cubeman and Batman.

Somehow Dad got the dinner on the

table without much help from anyone else, because he couldn't give any commands right. It was a strange-looking meal. The spaghetti swam in too much sauce. The garlic bread had jagged edges. The lettuce in the salad was torn wildly, as if by a madman.

Usually Dad was a great cook.

Reed thought this kind of meal was more interesting.

Everyone was quiet as the family sat down and took the first few bites. It took too much energy to think of the wrong things to say while they were eating.

And then Sukie knocked over her milk.

Reed saw Mom and Dad look at each other. Dad had panic in his eyes. Maybe he was fresh out of wrong things to say. Maybe he was scared he was going to say, "You've got to be more careful! Go get a towel and clean it up," no matter how hard he tried not to.

But Mom didn't look worried. She tossed her head, shaking the hair back from her face. And then, sounding as confident as an Olympic gold medalist, she said, "No, you can't have a snack. We're eating dinner in five minutes."

Sukie's eyes were big as she watched the pool of milk seep across the table. She seemed to be thinking hard. Reed held his breath, waiting for her comeback. Did she need help?

No—she was looking up now, staring straight into Mom's eyes.

"Reed got more than me," Sukie said bravely. You never would have known that milk was dripping through the crack in the table right into her lap. She flipped her hair over her shoulder, almost like a miniature version of Mom.

Dad burst out laughing.

"Ron! Stop it!" Mom hissed out of the side of her mouth. "You're going to undermine our authority!"

Dad laughed harder.

"A-Authority?" Dad said through his chuckles. "You just told your kid she couldn't have a snack because dinner's in five minutes. And we're already eating dinner. Where's the authority in that?"

Reed liked it that Dad thought this was funny.

"Yeah!" Reed said. "That was the best pair of wrong sayings ever. They were so wrong they almost made sense. Like, if Sukie had gotten as much milk as me, she could have spilled even more. And dinner's going to be stopped for five minutes because there's milk on everything, and somebody's got to clean it up. And wouldn't it be fun if we could have a snack in the middle of dinner?"

"Reed! Don't give away our strategy! They're not supposed to know we're doing this on purpose!" Brian whispered.

At the same time Mom hissed at Dad again, "Ron! The experiment!"

"The war!" Brian whispered. "We were winning—"

"They were about to cave! I know it!" Mom said.

Reed started giggling too. Mom and Brian were like two crazy generals. And he and Dad were like two fountains of laughter. Reed tilted back his chair so he could send a stream of laughter straight up into the air.

"Reed! Watch out!" Sukie yelled. "You're going to fall leaning back like that! Keep all four chair legs on the floor!"

And then Sukie clapped her hands over her mouth.

"Oops," she said. "I just did a parent-speak."

CHAPTER 13

EVERYONE TURNED on Sukie. Dad and Reed stopped laughing. Mom and Brian stopped glaring. Sukie shrank down in her chair. She didn't understand. Why was everyone looking at her?

"Young lady," Mom said slowly, "what did you just say to Reed?"

"Um, I told him not to fall," Sukie mumbled. "I told him to keep his chair legs on the floor. Just like, um, you always tell him."

"Aw," Brian growled. "You just ruined everything."

"I did not," Sukie said. She squirmed a little in her chair, so she could dodge the milk dripping from the table. "I probably saved Reed's life! He could have fallen over backward and broken his head."

Sukie saw that Reed was very, very slowly easing his chair down so it sat squarely on the floor.

"He wouldn't have fallen," Brian said. "He tilts his chair back all the time. He never falls."

"What if this time he did?" Sukie argued. "What if he broke every bone in his body and his brain squished out all over the floor?"

"Cool!" Reed said.

Sukie ignored him.

"And Mom and Dad weren't going to stop him. They weren't ever, ever, ever going to tell him to be safe," she said. "So I had to."

Dad wasn't looking at Sukie anymore. He was looking at Mom.

"Sukie's right," Dad said grimly. "We just endangered Reed with this stupid experiment."

"Oh, come on," Mom said. "He was just leaning back in his chair. It wasn't going to kill him."

Sukie, Reed, and Brian all stared at Mom. Their jaws dropped and their eyes bugged out in amazement.

"Then why do you yell at me about it all the time?" Reed asked.

"Because it's still rude and dangerous," Mom said. "A rule doesn't have to be life threatening to be important." She stood up and got a dishcloth from the sink. Then she started wiping up Sukie's spilled milk. Some of the milk still dripped onto Sukie's chair. But Sukie was glad to see that Mom cared again about cleaning up messes. Maybe Mom would even clean up the glitter hidden under the rocking chair.

Oh, no, Sukie thought. *What if I really do crave rules and order, like that magazine said?*

Well, she didn't ever have to admit it.

"The experiment's over, isn't it?" Reed asked sadly.

"Yep," Dad said. "I think we can call this one an unqualified failure." He stared down at the pool of spaghetti sauce on his plate.

"But it was fun," Reed said. "I liked everyone saying the wrong thing."

"It wasn't supposed to be fun," Mom said. "It was supposed to teach you a lesson."

She wrung the dishcloth out in the sink and came back to wipe up more milk.

"Mom," Sukie said. "We already *know* we're not supposed to spill milk, or run in the house or, um, play with glitter without permission—"

"Or kick soccer balls in the kitchen," Brian said.

"Or put handprints on the wall," Reed said.

"Or tilt back in chairs," Sukie said, glaring a little at Reed.

"So why don't you do what you're supposed to?" Dad asked.

"We just forget sometimes," Sukie said.

"Everyone makes mistakes," Reed said.

"How can we make sure you remember?" Mom asked. "How can we make you be careful?"

And it was strange. It was like Mom really thought Brian and Reed and Sukie could give her a good answer. Like she wanted their help.

"I know!" Reed said. "If you have to yell

at us, you could stop doing it the same way all the time. Be original. Don't say, 'No running with scissors.' Say, I don't know, maybe, 'Walk slowly when you have pointed cutting tools in your hands.'"

He looked around triumphantly.

"And by the time I'd figured out to say that, and actually said it, you'd have already tripped and stabbed yourself and I'd need to call nine-one-one," Dad said.

"Oh," Reed said.

Sukie saw what was going to happen. Mom and Dad were going to go back to yelling at them all the time, the normal way, just like usual. Nothing had changed.

Except . . . Sukie thought about how she'd felt, yelling at Reed about his chair. She'd really been scared that Reed would fall and get hurt. Did Mom and Dad feel like that all the time?

No wonder they yelled so much.

"But every once in a while, when you're not worried about having to call nine-one-one, couldn't you say *something* different?" Reed argued. "I'd listen more if I thought there was a chance you might say something interesting."

Dad laughed.

"I don't know," he said. "It's awfully hard for parents to be interesting."

"You could promise to try," Reed said hopefully.

"That's it!" Brian said. "We need a peace treaty."

"Huh?" Sukie said.

"A peace treaty. It's like, when a war ends, both sides sign a treaty saying they're not going to fight anymore," Brian said. "And the side that loses says it's going to give back land, or prisoners, or whatever.

And both sides promise to do things so there's not another war."

"Oh, please," Mom said. "This wasn't a war. And I'm not going to negotiate. Dad and I may not be interesting, but we are in charge. *We* set the rules."

She dropped the milk-soaked dishcloth into the sink with an emphatic plop.

"No, wait," Dad said. "This could be fun. Let's see what they come up with."

CHAPTER 14

So RIGHT AFTER DINNER Sukie, Reed, and Brian went to Brian's room to make up their peace treaty offer. It took a long time. First Brian wanted to write, "We, the victors of this war . . ." But Reed and Sukie told him that Mom and Dad would never sign something that said the kids won.

"Even though we *did*," Brian muttered. "Dad started laughing first."

He erased that sentence anyway.

Then Reed wanted to spell out all the imaginative, interesting, original things Mom and Dad could say.

"It's not original if you tell them what to say," Brian argued.

"Well, you don't think they're going to

come up with anything good on their own, do you?" Reed asked.

"Come *on*," Sukie said. "This is taking forever."

It was almost bedtime when the three of them walked out of Brian's room.

"Here," Brian said to Mom and Dad. He handed Mom their crumpled peace treaty. It had holes where Brian had had to erase so many times.

"'Roman numeral one. Brian, Reed, and Sukie promise to try harder to be good, if Mom and Dad promise not to yell so much or so boring,'" Mom read aloud. "You should say 'boringly,' not 'boring,' but so far this sounds good."

Dad read their second point over Mom's shoulder.

"Two. Mom and Dad will only yell about important stuff, and Brian, Reed, and

Sukie won't give the same old excuses all the time,'" Dad read. He glanced up, looking relieved. "I'm willing to sign this."

"There's one more thing," Reed said. "On the back."

Dad raised his eyebrows and turned the paper over.

Reed had written this one.

"'One day a month everyone will say all the wrong things again," Reed read aloud.

"I thought the point of a peace treaty was to end the war,'" Dad said.

"Mom said this wasn't a war," Reed said. "Please? Can't we do this just for fun?"

"And sometimes," Sukie said, "maybe the kids can say the parentspeak, and Mom and Dad can talk like kids."

She wasn't going to say the reason why. But telling Reed not to fall off his chair had made her think about how her parents felt.

Maybe if they had to talk like kids every now and then, they'd think about what it was like to *be* a kid.

Dad shrugged.

"I'm game," he said. "Sandy?"

"Oh, all right," Mom said. "Maybe one *night* a month."

"In that case," Dad said, "can we have dessert now? I'm *hungry.*"

His little-kid whine sounded really fake. He was going to have to work on that.

Sukie knew that she or Reed or Brian was supposed to say something like "But it's too close to bedtime," or "But you didn't eat all your vegetables at dinner," or even "Dessert's bad for you. Do you want lots of cavities?"

But Sukie was hungry too.

"Sure," she said. "Let's all eat cake!"

Everyone looked at Mom.

"All right," she said. "Just this once."

While they were eating the cake, Reed dropped crumbs on the floor and Sukie accidentally smeared icing on the table. And Mom and Dad didn't say a thing.

Then it was bedtime. And Brian didn't say "Aw, just five more minutes," and Reed didn't say "But I'm not tired!"

Probably it wouldn't last. But Sukie knew one thing as she snuggled into bed.

She couldn't wait for the next wrong-talking night.